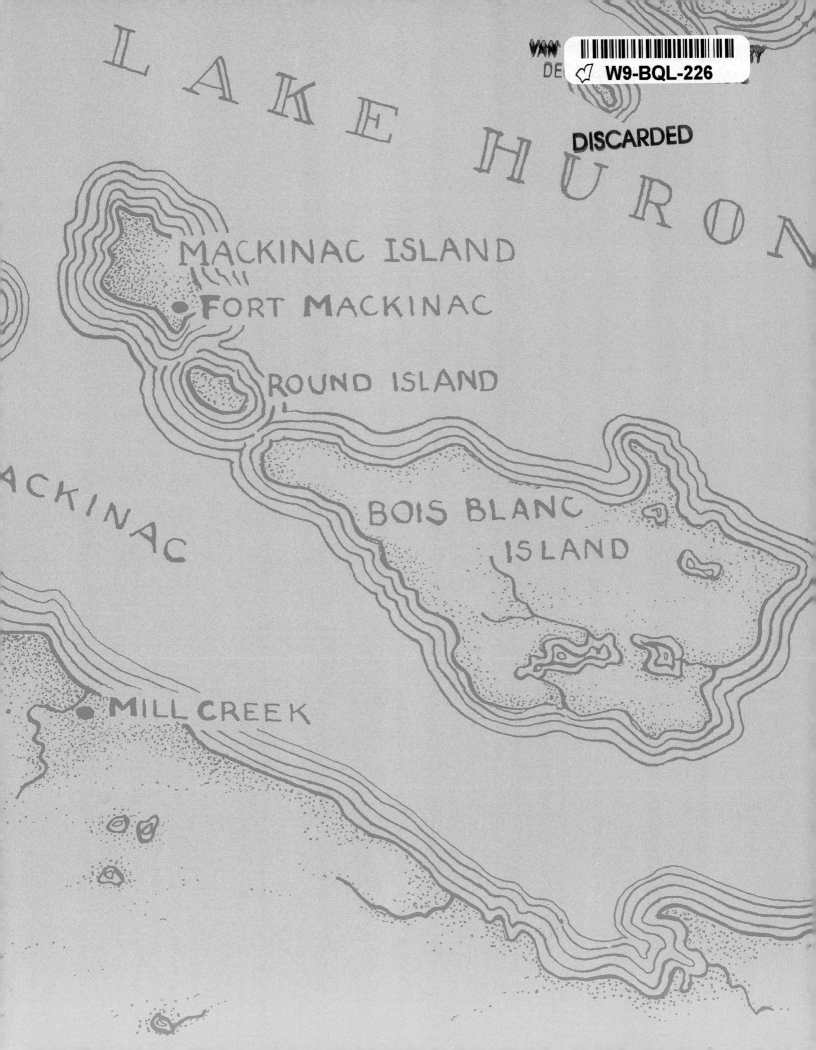

LAKE HURON

MACKINAC ISLAND
FORT MACKINAC

ROUND ISLAND

ACKINAC

BOIS BLANC
ISLAND

MILL CREEK

THE STORY
of
MICHIGAN'S
MILL CREEK

BY JANIE LYNN PANAGOPOULOS

ILLUSTRATED BY GIJSBERT VAN FRANKENHUYZEN

Sleeping Bear Press

MACKINAC
STATE · HISTORIC · PARKS

ACKNOWLEDGMENTS

My paintings require more than just paint, palette, and brush, and this story came alive for me through the talents of many people.

Thanks to Ron, Renee and Caroline Sherry for being the models for Papa, Mama and Little Mary Campbell. To complete the redheaded Campbell family, thanks to Jason Mahoney as James and Robert Cable as Johnny. I truly appreciate the long hours you all spent acting out each scene of the book.

Thanks to Durwood and Stephanie Shawl, who spent those hours encouraging their son-in-law and daughter (Ron and Renee) and granddaughter (Caroline) during the entire session. Also, special thanks to Stephanie for the costumes she created for the Campbell wardrobe.

Though you didn't know you were going to be in this book, thanks to Jim Evans, a tireless reenactor from Fort Michilimackinac, who has always been a valuable resource and model for my endless requests for information.

To Tim Harrigan, for spending several hours working with his magnificent oxen, and a special thanks to Mary Collisi, who arranged the ox-pull session.

Much appreciation goes to Carole and Ray Rewold, who answered all the questions I had regarding lifestyles and costuming of the era. Your knowledge is remarkable.

Thanks to Traie Shelhart, for taking the time to model as a British soldier, and Bill Smith, a reenactor from Mill Creek, who offered his time and expertise showing me the workings of the lumber mill.

I'd like to acknowledge the artistry of Victor Nelhiebel, whose illustrated overview of Mill Creek helped me recreate the Campbell's home and mill.

And finally, to Dave Armour, for allowing me to paint this book. I am very proud to be a part of this project.

—Gijsbert van Frankenhuyzen

Sleeping Bear Press
310 North Main Street
P.O. Box 20
Chelsea, MI 48118
www.sleepingbearpress.com

Printed and bound in Canada.

10 9 8 7 6 5 4 3 2 1

Library of Congress Cataloging-in-Publication Data on file.
ISBN: 1-58536-054-6

The job of an historical fiction author is to create a story blended with fact and fancy, and *A Place Called Home: Michigan's Mill Creek Story* is just that. It is designed to entertain you with a fascinating tale as well as to introduce you to this interesting historical location, held in stewardship by the Mackinac Island State Park Commission (MISPC).

The history of the inhabitants of the Straits of Mackinac dates back thousands of years to the indigenous people that once hunted, fished and cultivated this land. By the early 1600s, French fur-traders arrived from the east bringing with them their trade goods and culture. The early French settlers lived peacefully with the local Indians, and their joined presence, even today, can be felt at the reconstructed Fort Michilimackinac.

At the end of the Seven Years War (1754-1760), the French Government conceded rights at the Straits of Mackinac to British forces who first arrived there in 1761.

Later, during the American Revolution, the British demand for lumber in the Mackinac region soared (1779-1781). Afraid of an American attack at the Straits, the British moved their garrison to the island and built Fort Mackinac. Immediately before their relocation to the island, British Lieutenant Governor Patrick Sinclair recognized the need for a sawmill to be built in the region (1779).

In 1783, the Treaty of Paris forced the British to cede the Northwest Territory to the United States. But it wasn't until 1796, when American troops first came to Mackinac Island, that the residents of the Straits showed concern about their land claims. At that time, the United States Government established the Detroit Land Office to review those claims.

On October 19, 1808, a legal representative of Robert Campbell, "deceased," registered a claim at the Detroit Land Office for 640 acres located on the mainland south of Mackinac Island. This was the first official registration of the site. A map of the Straits, thought to have been created sometime between 1780-1790, clearly shows a sawmill built by Robert Campbell, an immigrant from Scotland, located on the bank of Mill Creek. Campbell decided upon this location, because it was the only river/creek in the Straits region with enough fall to generate the necessary waterpower, to drive the mechanics of a sawmill. Eleven years later, on March 12, 1819, Robert Campbell's heirs (John, Mary, and James Stevens) sold Private Claim number 334, the site of Mill Creek, to Michael Dousman of Mackinac Island for $1,000.

In 1881, a crew preparing a railroad grade at Mill Creek discovered a plaque bearing this inscription:

Here lieth the Body of
John Annan Late Corpl
In the 2nd Battn 60th Regt
Who departed this life feby 10
Anno Domini 1771
Aged 51 years

Checking British Muster Rolls revealed a Corporal John Annan from Fort Michilimackinac had indeed died February 10, 1771, lending more interesting history to the site.

The Commission and Mackinac Island State Park had its beginnings in 1895, and over the years was given the responsibility of developing, interpreting, and maintaining the historic sites of the Mackinac Region. In 1958, it became actively engaged in the restoration and interpretation of Fort Mackinac and Fort Michilimackinac, and took on the added responsibility of restoring the Old Mackinac Point Lighthouse.

In 1972, staff archaeologist Dr. Lyle Stone confirmed archaeological remains of what is known today as the earliest industrial site of the Northern Great Lakes Region—a saw and grist mill which served the needs of Fort Mackinac and the surrounding area. This site today is known as Historic Mill Creek.

Since few historical documents exist relating to Mill Creek, archaeological finds have proven to be the most important source of information available for this site. Archaeological evidence indicates that there was once a substantial community (approximately 1780-1840) at Mill Creek that held close ties to Fort Mackinac and Mackinac Island.

The mill and structures at Mill Creek today are accurate replicas used for historic interpretation.

"No, I'll not go! I'll not be crossin' the Straits of Mackinac again. Listen to that wind howlin'. 'Tis a warnin' I tell ya."

"Hush Robert Campbell, you'll be wakin' the children," said Mama with a whisper.

Little Mary and Johnny rubbed sleep from their eyes and pulled back the bearskin blanket from their bed. Quietly, they tiptoed across the loft and peeked down to see their father, mother, and older brother, James, sitting at the table of their cabin.

"I made an oath when I first came here from Scotland," said Papa, "to never leave this land or cross the open water again. This is our home here, I'll not leave it, nor give that wild water another chance at my life."

"Robert! Governor Sinclair has ordered everyone to leave Fort Michilimackinac and the old fort village. We must move to the new island settlement," insisted Mama. "We have no choice."

Little Mary and Johnny listened, their eyes growing wide when they heard they were to leave their home at Fort Michilimackinac.

"We Campbells are merchants, not sailors. We have no place there on that island of Mackinac. Drat those American patriots and their Revolution. I'll not be leaving my home for the likes of them. I have a plan, a plan that will please both Governor Sinclair and King George. A plan that will also keep us upon solid ground and not surrounded by water."

"Tell us!" urged James.

"Aye, tell us!" said Mama.

"There's land, not far from here, once cleared by soldiers for firewood, where maple sugar runs and a fine, swift creek flows."

"Aye," said Mama, "we know the place."

"It's there I'll build a sawmill to cut trees. This will please both the governor and king," said Robert Campbell proudly.

"Aye," said James, "it's said there's not enough wood on the island of Mackinac to build houses."

"Or to build churches and schools," added Mama.

"Nor for the buildings of the fort or cordwood for fireplaces," added Papa.

"Tis a good plan, Robert," said Mama with a smile.

Johnny and little Mary were pleased at how clever their father was. Carefully, they tiptoed back to bed, their father's voice fading into the howling winter wind.

Thick ice soon covered the Straits of Mackinac as the Campbells watched their neighbors, one by one, move to the new island settlement. Teams of horses and oxen, wearing spiked shoes, pulled large sleds filled with household items across the winter ice.

Soon the winter winds grew silent and splitting sounds
of cracking ice gave way to the warm spring.

Little Mary and Johnny watched as more families packed their featherbeds, shutters, and doors into boats that glided swiftly across the open water to the island of Mackinac.

Indian families, who made their homes in villages outside the old fort, soon filled their birchbark canoes with woven mats and rolls of bark from their lodges and paddled their canoes to their new island homes. Tears ran down little Mary's cheeks as she waved good-bye to her friends. Johnny wondered if he would ever see the bright red coats and fancy hats of the British soldiers or hear the happy notes of the voyageur's fiddle again.

Soon, old Fort Michilimackinac was empty and plumes of smoke rose high into the air above Mackinac Island from the fireplaces of the new settlement.

"Times a wastin'!" called Mama to Mary and Johnny. "Tis spring and we have a garden to plant. We will need lots of food when we move to our new home at Mill Creek."

Together, little Mary, Johnny, and Mama worked in the garden, planting corn, cabbage, potatoes, squash and beans.

One evening, Papa came home very happy. Governor Sinclair had finally given him permission to build a sawmill at the creek. "Mill Creek," said Papa, "that is what we will call it."

"Tomorrow we begin to build!" he announced proudly as he slapped James on the back.

"I want to help too!" demanded Johnny.

James laughed at his little brother. "You're too small to help," he said.

"No, Johnny isn't too small," insisted Papa, as he smiled proudly at his youngest son. "Johnny can help by looking after things here. There will be lots of work now that there is a cabin and sawmill to build. Johnny can chop firewood and bring water up from the lake for Mama. Johnny is not too small to work like a man. He's a Campbell!"

Johnny smiled at Papa and then scrunched up his face at his big brother.

The next morning, before the sun was even up, Papa and James left, carrying their tools to Mill Creek to begin their work on the new cabin and sawmill. They did this every morning for weeks.

In the garden at the old cabin, tiny plants began to grow taller and the summer days passed quickly.

One day, Mama gave little Mary and Johnny some crockery to carry and led them to the old apple orchard.

Mama carefully scooped up soil from around the roots of the apple trees and sliced off tender, new branches.

"These apple trees," she said, "were brought from across the great waters of the Atlantic Ocean to Mackinac, so mothers could feed their children to keep them healthy and help them grow strong. Let's plant these buds in crocks to take to our new home, where they too will grow strong to feed us."

Mama gently sprinkled water from her fingertips over the tiny new trees to help them grow.

One evening, Papa and James came home very excited and announced, "The cabin is finished! We have a new home!"

Everyone was happy. Papa danced around the cabin with Mama in his arms. James rolled up his sleeves, showing off his strong muscles from clearing land for the new cabin and sawmill. Johnny showed his muscles, too, from chopping firewood and carrying water.

The next morning, pots and dishes, featherbeds, and boxes of vegetables from the garden were all loaded into the oxcart. The chickens were packed into baskets and cattle brought in from the meadow. Carefully, Mama placed the crocks of young apple trees into the cart. Finally, it was time for them to leave Fort Michilimackinac and the old fort village, too.

Following an Indian trail along the lakeshore, the oxen slowly pulled the cart on the sandy trail. Their new home at Mill Creek was not far and soon they could see their new cabin in a sunny clearing in the forest.

Together the family lit the first fire in the cabin's fireplace and prayed for blessings and safekeeping in their new home and the sawmill that was to follow. Before the cows were led to the meadow to graze, James tied bells around their necks. Little Mary scattered grain to welcome the chickens. Mama carried the crocks filled with young apple trees from the oxcart and planted them in the dark, rich earth.

One day, soldiers came from the island in their bright red coats and fancy hats. Governor Sinclair had sent them because he needed lumber to build the new island fort. Papa was excited, but there was work to be done before wood could be cut at the new sawmill.

The soldiers stayed to help Papa and James. First they built a dam, like the beavers make, only bigger, to slow the swift-moving creek. With a dam, the water could be controlled.

Next, they finished the mill house that held the gears of the sawmill, and built a mill wheel. The mill wheel had paddles that would catch the water from the creek and turn the wheel round and round. When the mill wheel turned, gears in the mill house would move, and this would lift a great saw blade up and down to cut the wood.

Everyone worked very hard to build the sawmill at Mill Creek, the first of its kind near the Straits of Mackinac.

Orders were sent to the blacksmith on Mackinac Island to forge a large, sharp blade for the new mill to cut wood.

Soon a boat arrived from the island with the shiny new blade. It had many sharp, pointy teeth.

Papa, James, and the soldiers carefully fit the blade into place. The sawmill was ready!

Next, a door in the dam that blocked the water from flowing was opened, and through the sluice, water came splashing down on its way to the mill.

The fast-moving water caught the paddles of the great mill wheel, turning it slowly at first, then faster and faster.

Papa lifted a log into a carriage that was moved by gears. Those gears were moved by the mill wheel, which was powered by the force of the water of Mill Creek. It was now time to release the blade.

Suddenly, the mill house began to shake, making loud noises. Little Mary hid behind Mama's skirt and Johnny covered his ears.

The noise stopped and Papa and James appeared at the door of the mill house, smiling. "She's a fine mill," called Papa. "She's cut her first log!"

All the soldiers cheered and shouted "Huzzah!" They threw their fancy hats high into the air.

"So that is what a sawmill sounds like," said Mama.

"Aye," said Papa. "Each time the blade, lifted by the power of the water, bites into the wood, the mill shakes with the mighty power of the machine. 'Tis wonderful, is it not?"

Mama smiled at Papa, but Johnny knew Mama didn't think all that noise was so wonderful. Neither did he.

Soon, everyone got used to the sound of the noisy mill. Piles of sweet-smelling lumber were carried from Mill Creek to the shore of Lake Huron and loaded aboard boats or made into rafts to be floated across the Straits on their way to the island fort.

"My heart is glad to be on solid ground and have a fine new sawmill here at Mill Creek," said Robert Campbell to his family as they stood along the shore and watched their wood make its journey to Mackinac Island.

"Look Papa!" yelled Johnny, pointing his finger along the shoreline toward the old fort village. "Fire!"

"Oh Robert, the forest is ablaze!" cried Mama as little Mary clung to her Mama's skirts in fear.

"No," said James. "I heard the soldiers talking. 'Tis Governor Sinclair. He's ordered the old fort burned."

The Campbells watched as billows of dark-gray smoke filled the sky over the Straits of Mackinac.

Many people in canoes and boats from Mackinac Island drew near the shore to say good-bye to the old fort. A voyageur played a sad song on his fiddle as he sat in his birchbark canoe on the water. A cannon blast boomed and echoed from the island, giving a final farewell to the once proud fort of Michilimackinac.

Robert Campbell lifted little Mary to his shoulders and put his arm around his family, looking toward the island.

"It'll be a fine new fort and settlement," said James.

Mama wiped away tears from her eyes. "Aye, and new families will follow in need of schools and churches," she added.

"And new homes and buildings," said Johnny, "built of our wood from Mill Creek!"

Glossary

Barracks
a large building soldiers live in.

Birchbark Canoe
a canoe made from the bark of a birch tree.

Bearskin Blanket
a blanket made from the skin of a bear.

Beaver(s)
a soft-furred animal with strong teeth that lives both on land and in water. The beaver pelt was highly prized by fur-traders and the pelt was used to make hats.

Blacksmith
a man who works with steel over a forge.

Cordwood
a stack of cut wood, four feet high, four feet wide and eight feet long.

Crockery
earthenware household article.

Crock(s)
earthenware pots or bowls.

Dam
a barrier built across a river, stream, or creek to hold back and control the flow of water.

Drat
an exclamation, this is an old disguised oath. It is a corruption of the expression Rot it!

Forge
a workspace with a fire and anvil where metals are heated, pounded and shaped.

Fort
a fortified building used for military defense or protection.

Gears
a set of toothed wheels working together in a machine.

Governor
a person with authority who governs a province or state.

Governor Sinclair
(1736-1820) British Lieutenant Governor. Moved fort and settlement of Michilimackinac to Mackinac Island during the American Revolution.

Island Settlement
settlement on Mackinac Island formed when Fort Mackinac was built (1779-1781).

King
(King George the III) King of England during the time of the American Revolution.

Lodge
an Indian home made with bent poles and covered with tree bark.

Loft
a space under the roof of a house/cabin often used as a storage or sleeping room.

Lumber
trimmed logs sawed into planks.

Mackinac/Michilimackinac
In the 1700s Mackinac marked the point

between the settled East and the uncharted West. The name Michilimackinac is an Indian name meaning Great Turtle in reference to the humpbacked shape of Mackinac Island.

Maple Sugar
syrup made by boiling the sap of the maple tree.

Merchant
a storekeeper.

Mill House
a building fitted with machinery to grind/crush or cut a product.

Mill Wheel
a wheel driven by waterpower that turns gears located in a Mill House.

Oath
a solemn promise.

Old Fort Village
village at old Fort Michilimackinac.

OxCart
a cart that is pulled by an ox or oxen.

Ox
an adult castrated bull.

Patriot
a patriotic person loyally supporting their cause or country.

Revolution
to replace an old government with a new, such as: the American Revolution.

Robert Campbell
Scottish immigrant who came to Mackinac in the 1760s or 1770s. He built the first sawmill at Mill Creek.

Sawmill
a mill with a power operated saw that cuts timber into planks.

Scotland
Northern part of the Island of Great Britain.

Soldiers
members of an army.

Sluice
a passageway for water to flow from a dam.

Straits of Mackinac
Straits connecting Lake Huron and Lake Michigan; four miles wide at its narrowest point; site of Mackinac Bridge which connects Michigan's Upper Peninsula with Michigan's Lower Peninsula.

Voyageurs
men employed to transport goods and supplies from one fur trading post to the next.

Timeline
The Straits of Mackinac

11,000 Years ago:	Glacial ice leaves the Straits of Mackinac.
10,000 Years ago:	Native Americans arrive.
1634:	Nicolet arrives at the Straits and the fur trade begins.
1670:	Father Marquette builds a mission site for Huron tribe at Mackinac Island.
1671:	Marquette establishes a mission site at St. Ignace.
1690:	Fort DuBaude is established at St. Ignace.
1715:	French build Fort Michilimackinac.
1754-1760:	French and Indian War (Seven Years War).
1761:	British take control of Michilimackinac.
1763:	Ojibwa, Sac, and Fox Indians capture Fort Michilimackinac during Pontiac's Rebellion.
1764:	British return to Fort Michilimackinac.
1775:	American Revolution begins.
1779-1781:	Fort Michilimackinac and old village settlement abandoned and garrison moves to Mackinac Island.
1780s:	Robert Campbell builds Mill Creek sawmill.
1780s:	Fort Michilimackinac is burned under orders of Governor Sinclair.
1783:	American Revolution ends.
1796:	Fort Mackinac turned over to American troops.
1800-1808:	Gristmill built at Mill Creek.
1808:	Robert Campbell dies and his heirs inherit the mill.
1812:	British capture Fort Mackinac during War of 1812.
1814:	American soldiers defeated while attacking Fort Mackinac.
1815:	Treaty of Ghent-British return Fort Mackinac to American forces.
1819:	Mill Creek property and holdings sold to Michael Dousman.
1822:	Dr. Beaumont experiments on Alexis St. Martin.
1823:	Protestant Mission on Mackinac Island.
1836:	Treaty of Washington-Native American land sold to United States.
1839:	Mills at Mill Creek close.
1861-1865:	American Civil War.
1875:	Mackinac National Park created.
1895:	American troops leave Fort Mackinac and Mackinac Island State Park was created along with the Mackinac Island State Park Commission.
1957:	Mackinac Bridge is built.
1958:	MISPC starts to interpret historic sites on Mackinac Island.
1960:	Colonial Michilimackinac reconstruction begins.
1972:	Archaeological evidence is found at Mill Creek Site.
1984:	Historic Mill Creek opens to the public.